"Tomorrow is Thanksgiving," announced Miss Fowl, "and guess what you lucky students get to be thankful for?"

"The twenty-four-hour Ultra Lord marathon on TV!" yelled Sheen.

"No school!" said Jimmy.

"Pumpkin pie with lots of whipped cream!" cried Carl.

Miss Fowl shook her head. "No. You get to be in the Thanksgiving parade!"

They all groaned.

Miss Fowl held up two pilgrim costumes.

"Jimmy, you and Cindy will be Mr. and Mrs. Pilgrim this year," said Miss Fowl.

"I have to be married to Cindy?" Jimmy complained.

"I'm going to throw up," said Cindy.

Miss Fowl told Sheen and Libby they were going to be Native Americans.

Libby shook her head. "I can't wear these moccasins—they are *sooo* last year!"

"I'd rather be Ultra Lord and fight alien turkeys with my laser sword!" said Sheen.

"What about me?" asked Carl.

"You get to be a turkey!" said Miss Fowl.

Carl sighed. "I'd rather be a llama," he said.

Miss Fowl took them outside to practice.

"This is going to be the best Thanksgiving parade ever!" said Miss Fowl.

"This is going to be the worst day of our lives," Cindy mumbled.

"Don't worry," said Libby. "Nobody goes to the parade, so no one will see us."

Just then Butch and Nick walked by.

"Hey, Neutron, you and Cindy make a real cute couple!" Butch teased. "I always thought you were a turkey, Wheezer! Sheen, you look even dorkier than when you're in that stupid Ultra Lord costume!"

Nick smirked. "Libby, those moccasins are *sooo* last year!"

They walked away, laughing. "We're gonna tell everybody to come see you losers in the parade!" yelled Butch.

"We can't be in the parade like this," said Jimmy.

"Maybe we could make some stylin' new costumes?" Libby suggested.

"And write a Thanksgiving song!" said Cindy.

"Good idea," Jimmy said, smiling. "And I'm going to invent something that Butch and Nick and everybody in Retroville will never forget!"

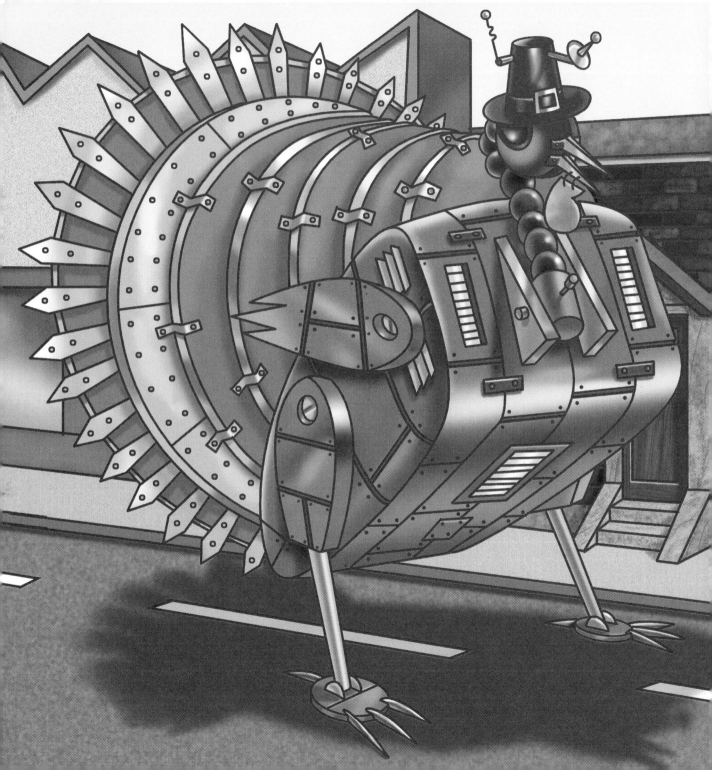

It was Thanksgiving morning, and the parade was about to begin.

"Ladies and gentlemen, I give you the Neutronic Robo-Turkey!" announced Jimmy.

"Jimmy, I knew you had that Thanksgiving spirit in you!" said Miss Fowl.

Carl held up a pie. "Anybody hungry? I brought some pumpkin pie!"

"No, thanks," said Jimmy. "That's sticky stuff. Better keep it away from the Robo-Turkey, or it could mess up the mechanism."

Cindy and Libby arrived wearing their new costumes.
"Nice outfits!" said Jimmy.
"Awesome robot, Jimmy!" said Libby.
Cindy shrugged. "It'll do in a pinch, I guess."
BRRRINNG! A bell rang. It was time for the parade to begin!

Jimmy walked beside the Robo-Turkey with the control in his hands. Cindy and Libby sang their song about giving thanks for family and friends coming together to celebrate. The crowd cheered!

Butch and Nick watched from the sidelines.

"Hey, what happened?" Nick asked. "The parade was supposed to be dorky, but it's sort of halfway cool!"

"Can I work the turkey, Jimmy?" begged Sheen.

"Me too!" said Carl.

"I guess it's okay," said Jimmy. "Just be really careful."

Sheen and Carl both grabbed the remote control and tugged on it.

"Careful, you guys!" shouted Jimmy. But it was too late. Carl and Sheen had broken the remote control.

The Robo-Turkey went berserk. It began to spark and twitch. Everyone ran for cover as the Robo-Turkey stomped through the crowd!

"Help!" cried Butch.

"We're being attacked by a giant turkey!" shouted Nick.

"He's headed for the Retroville stadium!" shouted Jimmy.
"They're playing the big Thanksgiving football game today,"
said Carl.

The Robo-Turkey stormed onto the field.

The crowd thought that the Robo-Turkey was part of the halftime show . . . until it started to chase the marching band and the football players!

The Robo-Turkey stomped out of the football stadium and headed for a neighborhood.

"We've got to stop it!" yelled Jimmy.

People ran out of their houses to see the giant Robo-Turkey.

Carl sniffed. "Mmm. I smell pumpkin pie."

"Carl, this isn't the time to be thinking about pie!" said Sheen.

Jimmy got an idea. "Yes, it is! Everybody! Bring out your pumpkin pies!" he shouted to the crowd.

All the people ran into their houses and came back out with pumpkin pies.

"On the count of three, throw your pies at the turkey!" commanded Jimmy. "One, two, three!"

WHOOSH! Everyone threw their pies.

The pies went into the Robo-Turkey's gears and mechanisms and jammed them up. The giant machine slowed down, sputtered, and finally fell over.

"That was awesome!" said Sheen. "Can we do it again next Thanksgiving, Jimmy?"

"Though a lot of pumpkin pie was wasted, I must admit that was the most exciting Thanksgiving parade we've ever had," said Miss Fowl.

"I sure am thankful the parade is over," said Jimmy.

Libby nodded. "We have a lot of things to be thankful for."

"Like we said in our song—family and friends," said Cindy.

"And don't forget pumpkin pie!" added Carl.